GROUNDWOOD BOOKS / HOUSE OF ANANSI PRESS

TORONTO  BERKELEY

AQUILES NAZOA

ILLUSTRATED BY ANA PALMERO CÁCERES

# A Small Nativity

TRANSLATED BY HUGH HAZELTON

With her husband at her side
sleepy and tired
María knocks on every door
in search of shelter.

"Don't worry, darling," José tells her.
"We'll see what happens.
I'm sure they'll let us in
when they know that you're expecting
and that our child is looking
for a bed to be born in."

The lovely Virgin shivers,
and he stops along the road
to take off his linen coat
and offer it to her.

"Come, my fairest damsel,
wrap this coat around you,"
he says with forced good humor
as he feels the mischievous cold
tugging at the holes
in his torn striped shirt.

From one door to another
they wander, humbly pleading,
and each time people answer
in just the same way:
"No boarders here, sir,"
or "How much can you pay?"

And in several houses
when they see María
someone jokes about her
and makes her blush.

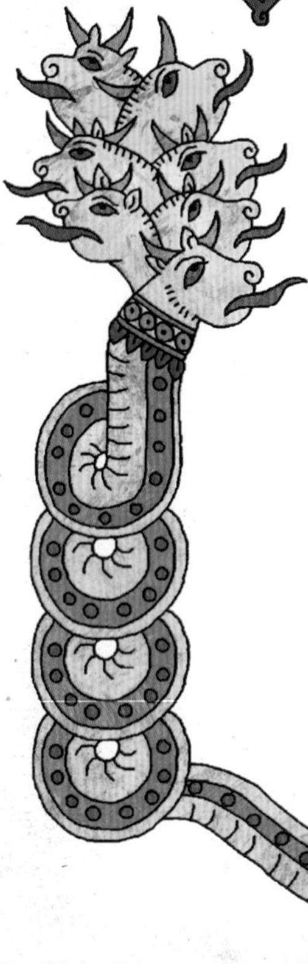

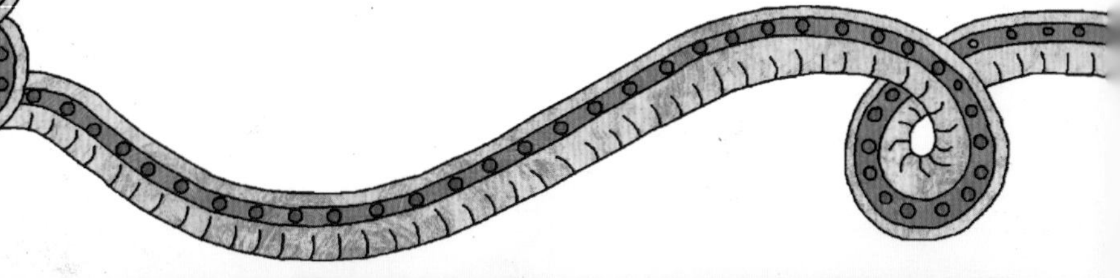

The poor couple!
There's no relief
from their sadness!
Everyone has a warm bed,
but no one has a heart.

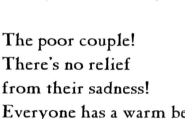

The Virgin is so tired and forlorn
that she begins to cry
and sadly turns to watch
how in the night, high and alone,
the moon is like a door
that opens wide.

At a shepherd's door
they finally knock:
all they ask for is a room
for the Lord to be born.
There's so much love inside
for the patient pilgrims
that the shepherd's wife
leaves off her weaving
and goes at once to bring them
cheese, bread and wine.

Now the Virgin spreads her coat
over the fragrant hay,
and like a slender rose
her saintly body bends.
A clear cry crosses the stable:
the ox's eyes turn toward her
and the donkey calls out too.

And they say
a silver star
shone that night on Bethlehem.

AQUILES NAZOA

ANA PALMERO CÁCERES

Born in Caracas on May 17, 1920, Nazoa was a poet and author renowned for the humorous intelligence and fine sense of irony that pervade his extensive body of work, which includes poetry, drama, stories, fables and essays. In 1948 Nazoa received the Venezuelan National Prize for Journalism given to folklorists and humorists. He died in 1976.

Born in Caracas on July 19, 1966, Ana Palmero Cáceres is a graphic designer and was Art Director at the noted Venezuelan publisher Ediciones Ekaré from 2000-2005. She has also worked in museums and art galleries, designing books and exhibitions and as a teacher of graphic design. Ana divides her time between the Canary Islands and Venezuela. This is her first book.

# ILLUSTRATOR'S NOTES

This book was inspired by the illuminated manuscripts that were created by monks in the Middle Ages, approximately 500 to 1500 years ago.

The word "monk" comes from the Greek *monarchos*, which means solitary.

My experience making this book brought me close to those long-ago monks who worked alone, creating exquisite miniatures on religious subjects. They worked from dawn to dusk, taking advantage of the sun's light. I felt as though I were in that special room, known as the *scriptorium*, filled with sheets of leather parchment for paper, inks, pens sharpened to a fine point by knives, pumice stones to smooth the parchment, rulers to draw lines and manuscripts propped up on lecterns. In my case, though, I had a lot of help from modern technology. First, I drew all the figures by hand, then I scanned them and, finally, I colored them digitally.

My work was influenced by these artists of the Romanesque period. I was inspired by early books such as codices, Bibles, missals and books of hours. And though I took liberties, my primary sources were two codices by the Holy Brother of Liébana and, especially, the codice by the Holy Brother of Girona.

Then I looked for traditional Christian symbols and combined them with elements that would bring together Nazoa's poem and the medieval style I had chosen. Since Nazoa is a Venezuelan author, I incorporated local flora, fauna, surroundings, clothing and *criollos*, or local people, into the monkish look of my art.

✳

### PAGES 2 and 3

The jaguar, which you can see through the leaves, represents a spiritual guardian. This is how the jaguar was seen by the first peoples of Central and South America.

✳

### PAGE 4

The Black cherub is the messenger for the text, which is about to begin. Cherubim are six-winged angels. They have two wings open above their heads, two below and two folded over their bodies. Their wings are often illustrated to resemble the wings of peacocks. Later, in the Renaissance, these cherubs were frequently depicted as little winged heads.

✳

### PAGES 6 and 7
#### (*With her husband at her side...*)

A cat is amongst the onlookers. He reminds us of the saying, "Curiosity killed the cat..."

✳

### PAGES 8 and 9
#### (*"Don't worry, darling," José tells her...*)

The spiral of flowers that begins in the sun and ends in Mary's womb shows how the birth of Christ binds heaven and earth. The spiral, a natural form, follows the same pattern as the creation of the universe. On either side of the double page are angels. Two of them carry the letters *Alpha* and *Omega*, the first and last letters of the Greek alphabet, symbolizing the beginning and the end.

The phoenix facing Mary and Joseph is a Christian symbol of the resurrection of Christ and life after death. It is also associated with fire and the sun. The phoenix can always be found near fire because it is reborn from its own ashes. The bird's red wings suggest the sun rising over the ocean, appearing anew each day.

✳

### PAGES 10 and 11
#### (*The lovely Virgin shivers...*)

The blue coat that Joseph wraps around Mary is decorated with the *fleur-de-lis*, which represents a lily. Both the color blue and the *fleur-de-lis* are traditional symbols for Mary.

✳

PAGES 12 and 13
(*From one door to another...*)

Here we find two representations of the battle between good and evil. On the left-hand page we see the celestial battle between the angel (heaven) and the devils (hell). The angel defeats evil by making the devils look at themselves in the mirror. On the right-hand page we find the earthly battle between Mary and Joseph (good) and the cruel gossip and rejection they faced from other people (evil).

✳

PAGES 14 and 15
(*The poor couple!...*)

Here again we find representations of evil and vice surrounding goodness.

On the left-hand page we can see the Seven Deadly Sins – Greed as a pig, Lust as a hare, Pride as a serpent, Avarice as a fox, Envy as a cat, Laziness as a monkey and Anger as a bear.

On the right-hand page three monkeys mime, "See no evil, speak no evil, hear no evil." They stand for those who ignore the poverty and needs of others.

✳

PAGES 16 and 17
(*The Virgin is so tired and forlorn...*)

The dove is often a symbol of the Holy Spirit, the third aspect of God in the Holy Trinity. A dove appeared to Mary with the angel Gabriel at the Annunciation.

✳

PAGES 18 and 19
(*At a shepherd's door...*)

The grape-laden vines represent both fertility (because they bear fruit) and sacrifice (because the grapes can be made into wine, which can be as red as blood). In Christ's birth his eventual death is foretold. A pot of sunflowers lines the entrance to the good shepherd's house. Because the sunflower always turns to face the sun, it symbolizes faith, devotion and constant love of God.

✳

PAGES 20 and 21

The border is illustrated with pineapples and oranges. Pineapples are associated with holiday celebrations. They are a traditional fruit for Christmas festivities and became a popular motif in eighteenth-century architecture, where they represented wealth and were considered a sign of welcome.

✹

PAGES 22 and 23
*(Now the Virgin spreads her coat...)*

On the left-hand page are the four evangelists: Matthew (angel), Mark (lion), Luke (bull) and John (eagle). They are each carrying the gospel that they wrote. They are standing on an object that appeared to the prophet Ezekiel in a vision. It is composed of a wheel within a wheel and is filled with eyes.

On the facing page is a pelican, a well-known allegory for Christ. People once believed that the pelican loved its children so much that it fed them its own blood. The border here symbolizes God as the Architect, as the Eye that sees all. The eye is found inside a triangle depicting God's vigilance and eternal justice.

✹

PAGES 24 and 25

The angel who brings the news of Christ's birth descends a ladder, another element that represents the unity of heaven and earth. He carries an olive branch in his hand as a sign of peace and the new covenant between God and man, which is fulfilled by the coming of Christ. The twelve sheep represent the twelve apostles.

✹

PAGES 26 and 27
*(And they say...)*

The circle evokes a dome, the vault of heaven. The angels are holding Venezuelan instruments – a four-stringed guitar, *maracas* and a harp.

✹

PAGES 28 and 29

The three kings are men from the great Venezuelan grass plains, and they are carrying their instruments. Their horses' saddles bear the letter for each of their names in Greek – Balthasar, Melchior and Caspar.

THE END

Text copyright © 1990 by Ediciones Ekaré
Illustrations copyright © 2007 by Ana Palmero Cáceres
English translation copyright © 2007 by Hugh Hazelton
First published in Spanish as *Retablillo de Navidad* by Ediciones Ekaré, Caracas, Venezuela, in 2007.
First published in English by Groundwood Books in 2007

Groundwood Books / House of Anansi Press
110 Spadina Avenue, Suite 801, Toronto, Ontario M5V 2K4
Distributed in the USA by Publishers Group West
1700 Fourth Street, Berkeley, CA 94710

We acknowledge for their financial support of our publishing program the Government of Canada
through the Book Publishing Industry Development Program (BPIDP).

Library and Archives Canada Cataloguing in Publication
Nazoa, Aquiles
A small Nativity / by Aquiles Nazoa; illustrated by Ana Palmero Cáceres; translated by Hugh Hazelton.
Translation of: Retablillo de Navidad.
ISBN-13: 978-0-88899-839-2 / ISBN-10: 0-88899-839-2
1. Jesus Christ–Nativity–Juvenile fiction. I. Palmero Cáceres, Ana   II. Hazelton, Hugh   III. Title.
PQ8549.N39R4813 2007   j863'.64   C2007-901649-9

Printed and bound in China

1075814127